CATMAGIC

For Sandra (and Puss)

— L.L.

Rupert, Toby and Spike, who helped model Izzy

Annick Press Ltd.

THE CANADA COUNCIL | LE CONSEIL DES ARTS
FOR THE ARTS | DU CANADA
SINCE 1957 | DEPUIS 1957

We acknowledge the support of the Canada Council for the Arts for our publishing program. We also thank the Ontario Arts Council.

Cataloguing in Publication Data
Lesynski, Loris
  Catmagic

ISBN 1-55037-533-4 (bound) ISBN 1-55037-532-6 (pbk.)

I. Title.

PS8573.E79C37 1998   jC813'.54   C98-930213-X
PZ7.L47Ca 1998

The art in this book was rendered in watercolour
  and coloured pencil.
The text was typeset in Utopia.

Distributed in Canada by:
  Firefly Books Ltd.
  3680 Victoria Park Avenue
  Willowdale, ON
  M2H 3K1

Published in the U.S.A. by
  Annick Press (U.S.) Ltd.
Distributed in the U.S.A. by:
  Firefly Books (U.S.) Inc.
  P.O. Box 1338
  Ellicott Station
  Buffalo, NY 14205

Printed and bound in Canada by Friesens, Altona, Manitoba

CATMAGIC

Written and illustrated
by Loris Lesynski

Annick Press
Toronto • New York

2

he Witches' Retirement Home has a room!"
said Arabelle Witch to the cat on her broom.

"After so many spells,
we need somewhere to stay."
She swooped to a stop and asked Izzy, "Okay?"

Izzy loved company.
Izzy loved talk.
He nodded a *YES!*
and they flew up
the walk.

GOOD WITCHES'
HOME
ROOM

3

The witch at the door said, "Please enter, my dear,"
then spied in the basket the tip of an ear.

"Ah ha, so you still have your standard black cat.
  What if he's troublesome, what about that?"

"We *must* be together," Witch Arabelle cried.

"We will see…" was the answer.
"For now, come inside."

But everyone saw,
    as they helped her unpack,
that Arabelle's cat wasn't
    standard *or* black.

Blotchy and splotchy
    from tail-tip to head,
two paws in purple,
    one amber, one red.

A jumble of crimsons
    and blues in a blur,
orange and yellow
    and limy-green fur.

The grin on his face clearly said:
    May I stay?
He niggled
    and naggled,
        paraded and haggled.
"All right," they agreed,
    "...but keep out
        of the way."

So Arabelle Witch and her Izzy
moved in,
eager for all of the fun to begin.

There was *everything* there—
except...
any space,
for each of the witches
had brought
to the place...

…her favourite cushions in dabbles and dots
…her favourite trinkets in spickles and spots.
Paisley amazingly
mingled with checks.
Curly things, swirly things
covered in specks.
So many sofas!
A mishmash of stuff!
So tired old Izzy
had choices enough,
and napped with an ear
always open to hear
the good conversation
delightfully near.

Until…

9

Ruby-Marie
   spilled her hot dragon tea.
She didn't see Izzy
   right next to her knee.

10

Then
Tall Ethel Tower
fell over him where
he was listening in
from a spot on the stair.

11

Griselda the Eldest was startled to find
Izzy flat and unhappy
behind her behind.

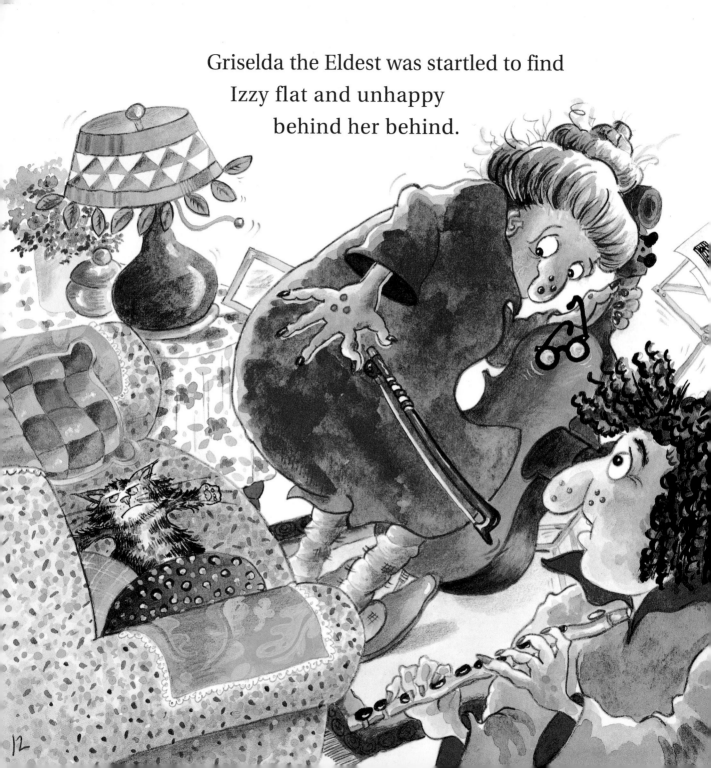

"We can't seem to see him!" the witches lamented.
So Izzy was tripped over, sat on, and dented.

"What if he stays in your room, out of sight?"
they asked Arabelle. But it didn't seem right.
"He *loves* to be with us," she firmly declared.
"He'll stay in the corner away over there."

14

Izzy *did* try…
  but he couldn't stay put.
In a minute again he was—
    underfoot.

"Somebody, soon," muttered Ruby-Marie,
  "is going to get hurt, and I hope it's not me."

"He simply must go," said the witches. "Too bad."
"Then I must go, too," whispered Arabelle, sad.

She started the packing while Izzy, below,
  shook his head: *No…I don't WANT us to go!*

15

Not safe on the sofa. Not safe on the floor.
But he'd never loved anywhere better before!

So...

he went to each witch and he wanted to know:
Any leftover magic from spells long ago?

"Oh, Izzy," protested Griselda,
 "we're old.
You couldn't do much
 with the magic
 we told.
A scrap of a spell,
 some ideas,
 that's all.
It's only the
 measliest bits
 we recall."

But Izzy insisted: *All bits would be good.*
    He niggled and naggled,
    persuaded and haggled,
'til every witch gave him the best that she could.

Cautiously, Izzy,
    the in-the-way cat,
signalled each witch
    to go gather her hat.
He beckoned them all
    to the shadowy hall.
He had a new spell:
    Are you willing at all?

They giggled a little,
    and mumbled some more
almost tripping on Izzy
    so close to the floor.

They said Izzy's spell.
    Nothing happened.
        Not then.

Eleven more tries.

    He persisted:
        AGAIN.

What did they whisper? What did they say?
What did they chant in that curious way?

Well, the very next second, they said, "WHERE'S THAT CAT?"
"He's not on the table. He's not on the mat."
"Look under the sofas!"
"Look under the beds!"
"Where is he?"
"*THERE'S* IZZY—

19

—over our heads!"

Yes! On the ceiling,
   spread out like a star,
Izzy was stretching
   as wide and as far
as any old cat who was
   safe and sound
   —as any old cat who was
   upside down.

"Look what
we did!" said Griselda.
"How clever!
Together our magic is
better than ever."
Ethel said, "Dear little
Izzy can stay.
He's still in the room—
but he's not in the way."

21

To feed Izzy crunchies, the witches would climb.

They stretched up to pat him at exercise time.

When Arabelle Witch missed her Izzy a lot,
Izzy invited her up to his spot.
A few bits of magic were saved just for this:
a visit with Izzy, a hug and a kiss.

And when anyone else wanted time on their own,

they magicked themselves to his upside-down home...

'til sometimes the ceiling
was so full of *them*…

28

Izzy became
right-side up
once again.

• THE END •